THE DINOSAUR DISCOVERY

Also by Laura James

illustrated by Églantine Ceulemans

Captain Pug
Cowboy Pug
Safari Pug

illustrated by Emily Fox

Fabio the World's Greatest Flamingo Detective:
The Case of the Missing Hippo
Fabio the World's Greatest Flamingo Detective:
Mystery on the Ostrich Express

illustrated by Charlie Alder

The Daily Bark: The Puppy Problem

THE DINOSAUR DISCOVERY

LAURA JAMES · illustrated by CHARLIE ALDER

BLOOMSBURY
CHILDREN'S BOOKS
NEW YORK   LONDON   OXFORD   NEW DELHI   SYDNEY

BLOOMSBURY CHILDREN'S BOOKS
Bloomsbury Publishing Inc., part of Bloomsbury Publishing Plc
1385 Broadway, New York, NY 10018

BLOOMSBURY, BLOOMSBURY CHILDREN'S BOOKS, and the Diana logo are trademarks of
Bloomsbury Publishing Plc

First published in Great Britain in March 2022 by Bloomsbury Publishing Plc
Published in the United States of America in May 2022 by Bloomsbury Children's Books

Bloomsbury books may be purchased for business or promotional use. For information on bulk
purchases please contact Macmillan Corporate and Premium Sales Department at
specialmarkets@macmillan.com

Library of Congress Cataloging-in-Publication Data
available upon request
ISBN: 978-1-5476-0955-0 (hardcover) · ISBN: 978-1-5476-0954-3 (paperback)

Printed and bound in China by C&C Offset Printing Co. Ltd, Shenzhen, Guangdong
2 4 6 8 10 9 7 5 3 1

To find out more about our authors and books visit www.bloomsbury.com
and sign up for our newsletters.

The doors closed, the whistle blew, and the city train at Platform 1 of Puddle Station left perfectly on time. Bob wagged his tail. He felt sure there was nothing in the whole world he'd ever love more than trains.

Colin, the stationmaster, bent down and gave Bob a tickle behind his ear. Trains and his master, decided Bob as he trotted beside Colin.

"Who's a good boy?" Arjan, the station cafe owner, called out, and Bob came running for the biscuit he knew Arjan had in his hand.

Trains, Colin, and treats from the cafe.

Contented, Bob sat down as Colin and Arjan passed the time of day.

After a short while Bob gave a little whine. When that was ignored, he tugged gently on Colin's trouser leg. The next train was due in.

"Bob's reminding me the branch-line train is coming," Colin said. "Don't tell anyone, but he's the boss around here!"

Arjan laughed and they all got back to work. Bob checked as Colin secured the tracks in time for the train's arrival. It too pulled in perfectly on time. This pleased Bob a great deal.

But a few moments later, Bob spotted a problem. The branch-line train had pulled in on time, but it was now a whole minute late leaving. He went over to see why the train driver hadn't closed the doors.

At the far end of the train, Mr. Marcus—a man Bob recognized as the owner of the Curiosity Shop—was looking angry. He was struggling to get something onto the platform. Bob barked the alarm and rushed over to see if he could help.

Mr. Marcus was pulling on a dog leash. When Bob got nearer, he realized that standing in the doorway of the train was the most extraordinary dog he had ever seen. The dog had long sleek fur and a

 sparkle in her eye. She was the color of his favorite chew toy and she smelled like hay.

This dog was peering nervously into the gap between the train and the platform edge.

"Come on, you stupid dog, move!" Mr. Marcus yelled.

Bob was shocked at such rudeness and, besides, it was clear that fear had set in and no amount of yelling would convince this dog to get off the train.

Bob boarded the train and stood beside her. He followed her gaze

down into the gap. He remembered
a time when he too was frightened
of the gap between the train and
the platform.

"It's not as bad
as it seems," he
assured her.

She looked
at his short
legs and
then her
long ones.

"If I can make it safely onto the platform," Bob said, "then you definitely can."

She raised an eyebrow.

"Okay, watch this." Bob jumped from the train onto the platform. "Easy!" he said, jumping back onto the train. "Look, I

can even skip it!" He did so and she gave a small wag of her tail.

"Now you try," he suggested. "Easy. Jump off. Easy. Jump on. Easy." Bob got a little carried away jumping on and off the train. So much so that he didn't notice she'd already elegantly stepped off the train and was safely on the platform.

The whistle
blew, and Bob had
to leap quickly
back onto Platform 2
before the doors
closed and he
was taken to the
next station.

Mr. Marcus was hurrying the
extraordinary dog away, but before
she left the station she glanced
back at Bob.

"I'm Diamond, by the way," she called out.

What a morning, thought Bob.

At that afternoon's Daily Bark news briefing, Bob was finding it difficult to think about anything other than Diamond.

Gizmo, as editor-in-chief, chaired the meeting. "We really need a big story.

Bunty, what have you got?" he asked. "What's the weather going to be like?"

"Sunny with occasional showers," Bunty replied confidently. Being a farm dog, she understood the importance of knowing the forecast.

"Lola, any sports news?"

"Yes," Lola replied excitedly.

"Swimming in the river is back! Someone has kindly removed the shopping cart that was littering the riverbank, so the access is all clear. I'd like to encourage everyone to make a splash! And remember, stand as close to your humans as possible when shaking yourself dry. They love that. In other news, Jackson the goldendoodle has broken the Puddle record for squirrels chased in one walk—a whopping fourteen! The squirrel season is particularly good this year."

"Thank you, Lola. And Bruno?"

Bruno gave the News Hounds  the low-down on the latest flea treatment. His report made Bob itch.

He wondered if Diamond ever got fleas. *Probably not*, he decided.

"Bob? Have you got any travel news to share?" Gizmo was asking him.

"Oh, sorry, yes." Bob snapped out of his daydream. "There will be a freight train coming through at midnight tomorrow. It'll be noisy, but tell residents there's no need to bark unless they want to."

"Thank you, News Hounds. Not exactly the big scoop I was hoping for, but we'll see what we can do with this."

Bob could tell that Gizmo was eager to close the meeting

and start work on the layouts,
but he couldn't help himself . . .

"Does anyone know anything
about the new dog in town? Her
name's Diamond," he blurted out.

It was Jilly who answered first.
As the Daily Bark's lead

reporter, she
always knew
the latest social
news in
Puddle.

"Apparently she came as part of the contents of a house sale Mr. Marcus attended. Her human could no longer keep her and told Mr. Marcus he couldn't take the contents of the house for his shop without taking her too."

"That's very sad," said Bob.

"The really sad thing," said Jilly, lowering her voice, "is that he doesn't even like dogs. The rumor is he's a cat person."

The News Hounds gasped in
unison.

"Poor Diamond," murmured Bob.

"I met her this morning," said
Gizmo. "She seems very nice."

"I'd like to be her friend," said Bob
a bit too loudly, and suddenly he felt
like everyone was staring at him.

"You could go to Pageant Gardens
tomorrow," said Gizmo. "Mr. Marcus
has started walking her there at
eleven o'clock every day."

The following morning Bob
bounded out of his basket and
barked to be let out (a little earlier
than Colin would have liked). He
felt full of energy.

It was a busy morning at the

station, and Bob was in the signal box when Diamond's train arrived. He was filled with great satisfaction as he watched Diamond step off the train without hesitation.

Once the morning rush hour was over, Bob slipped out through the ticket office and carefully went over the crossing. Colin could manage the station on his own for a little while.

Pageant Gardens was a short

walk away. Bob sniffed the air happily. Unfortunately, Bunty's latest weather forecast was spot on. One of her "occasional showers" arrived. The heavens opened and Bob ran for the cover of the bandstand. As he did so, a little mouse with a similar thought scurried right under his nose and darted into a hole between the bandstand's old, rotting boards. Bob's terrier instincts, never far from the surface, sprang into action and he began to dig and claw at the decaying wood, which broke away easily.

His clumsy scrabbling gave the mouse plenty of time to get away, but it took Bob a while to realize it was gone and that the rain had stopped. He shook himself and looked around. He felt a bit embarrassed. He'd made the hole in the floorboards a lot bigger.

Just as he was trying to cover up the mess, he noticed Diamond and Mr. Marcus enter the park.

Bob straightened himself up and gave his fur a quick sniff. Damp dog. Excellent.

He was about to head over and introduce himself when he noticed nearly half the dogs of Puddle were doing the same. Diamond was clearly already very popular.

Bertie, the vet's Labrador, was

carrying a stick, which he dropped at Diamond's feet. Diamond wasn't able to stop and appreciate it because Mr. Marcus was pulling her leash so hard.

Bob wondered if it was Diamond's birthday just as Rosa, a chihuahua, dropped a tennis ball in Diamond's path. *I should get her a present!* Bob decided.

Bob dashed back to the bandstand. *Perhaps she'd like the mouse*, he wondered. *No, I don't want her thinking I'm a cat.* Bob glanced around. *A bit of bandstand floor? No, that isn't good enough.*

Fortunately, inspiration struck, and Bob dived into the Bob-sized hole he'd made in the floorboards. Most of the good things he had found in life were buried, he remembered, so he started digging in the soft earth. And with a bark of delight he unearthed a bone.

She'll love this, he thought.

The bone was much bigger than the hole Bob had made in the floorboards, and it took quite an effort to retrieve it. When he finally got it out and looked around for Diamond, he realized she had left the park.

In his disappointment, Bob took a step back and fell through the hole in the floorboards.

Ouch!

Once he had dusted himself off, however, he found to his astonishment that there wasn't just one bone under the Pageant Gardens bandstand—there was a whole pile of bones. And they were the biggest, juiciest bones he'd ever seen!

This was the scoop of the century!
Bob carefully put the bone back
where he'd found it and ran flat
out to Gizmo's house.

"Gizmo, Gizmo! Hold the front
page!" he barked. "I've got a story

for you. A big one. In fact, the most amazing story Puddle has ever known!"

It was a bold claim, but as Bob spat out the story in an excited jumble, Gizmo grabbed his camera. "We'd better get Jilly!" he said.

Jilly was just as excited at the news of the big scoop, and the three of them rushed to Pageant Gardens.

When they reached the bandstand, Bob busily removed some of the

floorboards and then stood back.
"Ta-da!" he said proudly.

Gizmo and Jilly peered under
the bandstand floor in awe. Jilly
quickly started taking photos.

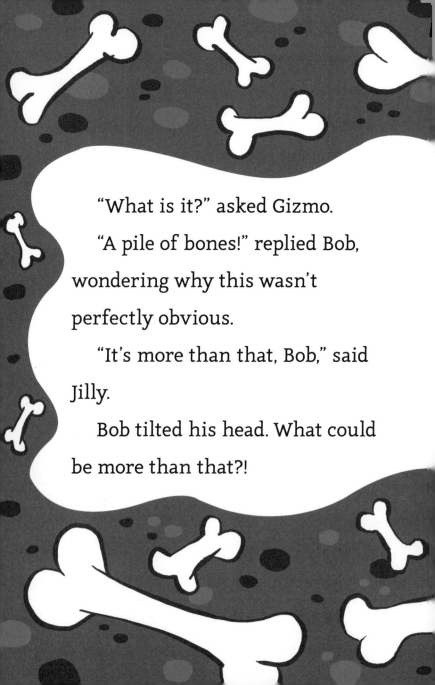

"What is it?" asked Gizmo.

"A pile of bones!" replied Bob, wondering why this wasn't perfectly obvious.

"It's more than that, Bob," said Jilly.

Bob tilted his head. What could be more than that?!

"It's a skeleton," Gizmo informed him. "You've found a skeleton under the bandstand."

Bob took a closer look and then sat back on his haunches in amazement. "Of what?" he asked finally.

"A big dog, perhaps?" asked Gizmo.

"A big dog?!" said Jilly. "When have you ever seen a dog that big?"

Bob and Gizmo looked up at Jilly's towering form but decided not to say anything.

"I think it's a horse," she suggested.

"I think it's a hippo," said Gizmo. "Look, you can just see its head there . . ." He twisted his body around to get a better look.

"Poor hippo," said Bob, bowing his head in respect.

"Why on earth would a hippo be buried under the Pageant Gardens bandstand?" asked Jilly, her mouth salivating. A ribbon of drool fell on to Gizmo's head. "Sorry," she apologized, licking her lips. "All these bones are making me hungry."

Gizmo shook it off. "No worries," he told her, flapping his ears.

"All the recent rain must have uncovered it," observed Jilly.

This was a once-in-a-lifetime discovery. Gizmo's journalistic instincts began to kick in. "We mustn't let anyone else know about this, not until we break the story," he instructed them. "Jilly, we need to get back and get writing. Well done, Bob.

You're right—this *is* the scoop of the century. But remember, it's top secret!"

As Gizmo and Jilly sped off, exchanging possible headlines as they went, Bob felt a moment of pride. He couldn't believe his own good fortune, and all he wanted to do was tell Diamond about it. It was then that an idea struck him—one which made him feel even happier.

There were so many bones,
surely one wouldn't be missed.
Ignoring a twinge of guilt, he

dug into the earth and retrieved
the biggest piece of skeleton he
could carry.

4

CANIS MIRABILIS

When Bob got to the Curiosity
Shop, Diamond was asleep in her
basket and Mr. Marcus was taking
stock at the back of the shop.

Bob couldn't open the door, so he
decided to push the bone through

the mail slot. It wasn't easy and it jammed halfway through. A quick glance at the shop's clock told him he had to hurry back to the station, so he left the bone where it was and ran back to work.

He arrived at the station just as Colin was blowing his whistle to signal to the driver of the train on Platform 1 that it was safe to depart. And, just like that, Bob had a new plan to meet Diamond.

It took Mr. Marcus over an hour before he noticed the bone hanging through the shop's mail slot.

"What's this disgusting thing?" he asked, looking around. But he couldn't see anyone, so he brought the bone into the shop and threw it in the wastepaper basket, muttering something about litterbugs.

Mr. Marcus's Curiosity Shop had been part of Puddle village for many years. It was filled with all kinds of peculiar objects. Some of them gave Diamond the creeps. In one corner there was a collection of stuffed rats. In another there was an array of headwear, ranging from masks to war helmets. The air was musty and nearly every surface was covered in dust.

Mr. Marcus went back to his seat

behind the shop counter and tried to tally yesterday's earnings on the back of an envelope. Business was slow.

While he was occupied, Diamond inspected the strange bone that Mr. Marcus had discarded. It didn't smell like any bone she'd come across before. She wondered where it had come from. She turned to Mr. Marcus's bookshelves.

The shelves were filled with

vegetable-growing manuals,
how-to-paint-in-watercolor books,
and hundreds of atlases. Finally
she found a book that might just
help her.

When Mr. Marcus went to make
himself a cup of tea, Diamond
nosed the book off the shelf and
perused its pages. She examined
the pictures and compared them
with the bone. It was then that
the truth jumped out at her. She

couldn't quite believe it, but the
picture on page fifty-five was a
perfect match.

She didn't have time to take this in before the shop bell rang. Thinking quickly, she sat on the book to hide her discovery. As the customers came in, Diamond recognized the stationmaster and the dog who had helped her off the train. She wagged her tail in greeting and the dog padded over to her.

"I'll be there in a sec," Mr. Marcus called out to Colin, putting his tea to one side.

Bob was thrilled that he was finally able to introduce himself to Diamond, and relieved he'd practiced it. "I'm Bob," he said.

"Hi, Bob," replied Diamond.

"That's Colin, my human," he added. "His whistle doesn't work. I dropped it in my water bowl on purpose so I could see you."

Colin was explaining to Mr. Marcus how some rainwater had gotten into his whistle and now he needed a new one. Mr. Marcus was eager to make a sale and pulled out a tray full of every type of whistle you could imagine—from dog whistles to ship's whistles—for Colin to inspect. There was even a selection of harmonicas and bugles. Colin decided he'd like to try them all.

The din gave Diamond and Bob the perfect cover to discuss the bone.

"Was it really from you?" Diamond was clearly impressed.

"I thought it must be your birthday," said Bob. "All the other dogs in the park were giving you gifts, and I hadn't gotten you anything."

"It's not my birthday," said Diamond. "I don't know when my birthday is, as it happens. I was a rescue pup, and so my owners didn't know when to celebrate it. And now, well, I don't think Mr. Marcus is really into birthdays."

Bob thought this was very sad, but before he could comment she changed the subject.

"Do you know what it is?" she asked.

"It's a bone," he replied, wondering why everyone kept asking him such obvious questions.

"Yes, but it's not just any bone," she said, showing Bob the illustration in the book.

"It's a dinosaur bone!"

Bob's eyes nearly popped out of his head and he accidentally gave a little bark.

"Won't be long now, Bob," Colin assured him. "He gets very anxious if he's away from the station for too long," he explained to Mr. Marcus.

But for once Bob wasn't thinking about trains. "You really think it's a dinosaur bone?" he asked.

"A young dinosaur, I think,"
said Diamond. "Where on earth
did you find it?"

"Underneath the bandstand
in Pageant Gardens. I
was chasing a mouse."

"Incredible," said Diamond.

"Thanks," replied Bob. "I'm
usually quite good at chasing
things. But this one got away . . ."

Bob realized this wasn't really
what Diamond had meant.

"Were there any more bones?"
she asked.

"Yes! We found a whole skeleton,"
Bob informed her. "It's top secret.
Until Gizmo breaks the story in
the Daily Bark."

"I've met Gizmo," said Diamond.
"He told me all about your newspaper."

"We call ourselves the News
Hounds," Bob said proudly. "I'm the
travel correspondent. I must tell
Gizmo about this new development.

He'll be really impressed. I'll make sure you get a mention."

Just then, Bob and Diamond felt a shadow fall over them.

It was Mr. Marcus. Colin was waiting for Bob by the door.

"Come on, we need to get back in time for the four fifteen," Colin reminded him.

Bob followed his master, giving a shy wag of his tail as a goodbye to Diamond.

As soon as they'd left, Mr. Marcus rubbed his hands together. He loved making a sale. Then, looking down at Diamond in disgust, he shouted, "You're getting in the way again." He shooed her off to her basket. She avoided his boot and slunk away, but she didn't have a chance to hide the book and the bone! Mr. Marcus spied them and Diamond's heart sank.

His expression changed as he glanced over the pages. He reached for his phone and his words filled Diamond with dread.

"Hello, is this the museum?"

5

CANIS MIRABILIS

Bob was thrilled to see his picture in the Daily Bark the following morning. He felt a bit like a celebrity. He'd managed to tell Gizmo of Diamond's dinosaur discovery just before the paper went to print. He hoped Diamond would be really happy to see her name in the newspaper. He tucked his copy of the paper under his blanket and went off to check if Colin had changed the signals correctly.

Diamond was on her usual train and Bob dashed over to see her.

"Did you see the paper? You got a mention . . ." he blurted out.

Mr. Marcus was pulling

Diamond on her leash and Bob was having difficulty keeping up.

"He knows," Diamond said under her breath.

"Who knows? Who knows what?" asked Bob, a little confused. He'd expected Diamond to be happier than this.

"Mr. Marcus knows it's a dinosaur bone. He's going to sell it. And the museum wants to know where he found it!"

"But he doesn't know where we found it," replied Bob.

"He's stopped feeding me in the hope I'll lead him to the bones," she whined as Mr. Marcus dragged her over the tracks.

The barriers fell just as Bob was about to follow her.

Poor Diamond! he thought.

As he sat waiting for the barriers to lift again, he decided he'd have to tell Gizmo.

Bob raced to the Daily Bark's headquarters (aka Gizmo's house) and was relieved to see both Gizmo and Jilly were there.

It had been quite a run, but in between pants Bob explained everything.

"I know I shouldn't have taken that bone to the Curiosity Shop," said Bob, shamefaced.

"But if you hadn't," Jilly pointed out, "we wouldn't have found out it was a dinosaur bone."

"No use crying over spilled kibble," said Gizmo. "What we have to do now is move the skeleton! Bob, get back to the shop and make sure Mr. Marcus stays inside until we're done."

So, as Jilly and Gizmo sprang into action, Bob ran for the Curiosity Shop with one of his favorite treats.

It was nearly dark when Bob peeped
through the window. Diamond was
lying sadly in her basket.

He whined a high-pitched kind of whine that only dog ears can pick up. Diamond jumped to her feet and opened the door—just enough to let him through, but not so much that the shop doorbell would ring.

"I've brought you something to eat," he told her, placing the treat at her feet.

"Ooh, thank you," said Diamond, wolfing it down without really chewing.

"Jilly and Gizmo have gone to move the skeleton," Bob told her.

Diamond nearly choked on the last bit of treat. "Oh no!" she gasped. "Mr. Marcus is getting ready to go skeleton-hunting right now.

What if he sees them? I've heard
him on the phone to the museum.
If he finds the whole skeleton,
they've promised him lots of
money. Then he'll leave Puddle
and take me with him!"

"You can't leave Puddle!" said
Bob. "You only just got here."

For a moment Diamond looked
as if she might howl in misery,
but then a look of steely resolve
came into her sparkly eyes.

"We can slow him down," she said. She whispered her plan in Bob's ear.

A moment later, Mr. Marcus walked into the dark shop, ready for his dinosaur hunt.

At a nod from Diamond, Bob darted behind a bookcase and then scrambled onto an old chair. On top of

the bookcase
was a record
player. He set
it playing at
full volume.
"What?
Who's there?!" Mr. Marcus shouted,
waving his arms around in the
dark.

Then Diamond climbed into
an old rain poncho and ran
toward him.

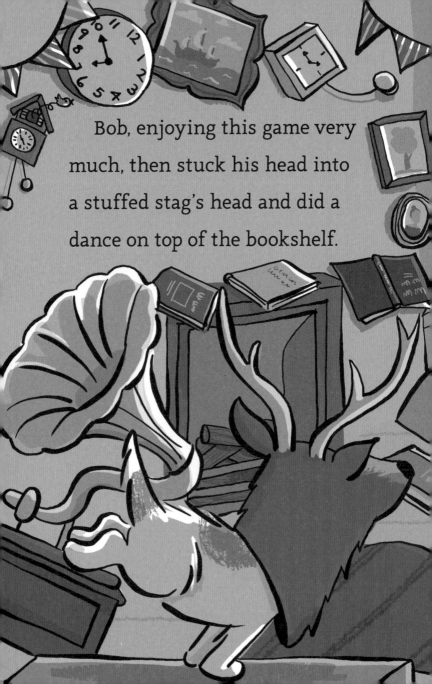

Bob, enjoying this game very much, then stuck his head into a stuffed stag's head and did a dance on top of the bookshelf.

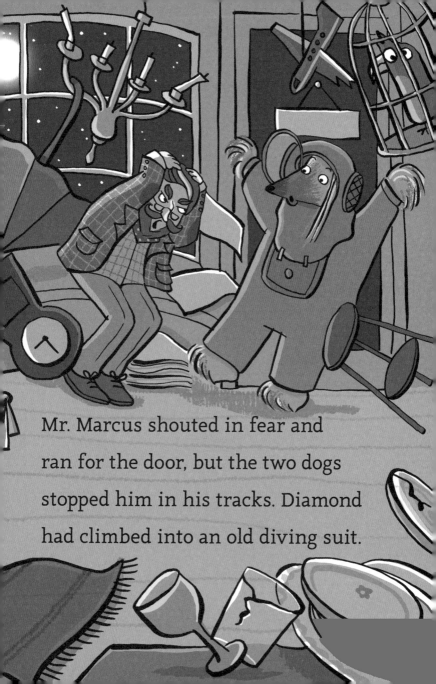

Mr. Marcus shouted in fear and
ran for the door, but the two dogs
stopped him in his tracks. Diamond
had climbed into an old diving suit.

Mr. Marcus was terrified. He cowered behind the shop counter.

Diamond and Bob were an excellent double act, and things were going really well until Mr. Marcus unexpectedly lunged forward. He caught hold of Bob's tail and put him in an antique birdcage, complete with stuffed parrot.

Diamond, dashing to his rescue, was cornered. Mr. Marcus managed to grab hold of her collar and tie her to a rocking horse. They were trapped.

Meanwhile, under the cover of darkness, Jilly and Gizmo had gone door to door enlisting the help of all the dogs in Puddle. Once they'd gathered the troops, Jilly instructed them to select a dinosaur bone each and form an orderly line.

The dogs were eager to help and began digging and picking dinosaur bones that were just the right size for them to carry. They waited fairly patiently (some being more obedient than others) for Jilly's command.

"Follow me!" she ordered. "Don't be seen. And strictly no chewing."

The dogs carried the bones in formation so that it looked like the dinosaur skeleton had come to life and was taking a stroll down Puddle's high street.

Suddenly Jilly heard a commotion, followed by the ring of the Curiosity Shop doorbell.

Mr. Marcus, brandishing the first dinosaur bone, burst onto the street.

Jilly signaled for the dogs to stop and take cover. They did the best they could, hiding in bushes, behind garbage cans, and at the bus stop. But some were better at it than others.

Mr. Marcus took in the extraordinary scene. "There's a whole skeleton! I'm going to be a millionaire!" he exclaimed.

But Bob and Diamond hadn't given up. Bob rolled the antique birdcage so that he and the stuffed parrot, like two hamsters in a wheel, barreled through the open shop door, knocking Mr. Marcus off his feet.

Diamond followed him, heaving the rocking horse behind her.

Jilly gathered her troops and headed out of danger.

Bruno, Lola, and Bunty broke formation and sat on Mr. Marcus while Jilly ordered the rest of the dogs to keep moving.

The door of the birdcage had opened and Bob wriggled out. He then freed Diamond.

They looked at Mr. Marcus. "What do we do now?" asked Diamond. "They can't sit on him forever."

Bob looked at the town-hall clock. "I've got an idea," he told Diamond.

"Let him go!" he told Bruno, Lola, and Bunty. They were so surprised that they tumbled off and Mr. Marcus struggled to his feet.

With one angry look at the
dogs, he ran in the direction the
skeleton had gone.

"What are you doing?" asked
Diamond. "He's going to catch up
with them!"

"It should be okay,"
replied Bob, chasing after
Mr. Marcus. "As long as
everything's on time!"

As the station came into view, they saw that the Puddle dogs and their dinosaur treasure had made it safely over the tracks, but Mr. Marcus was hot on their tails.

Being small, Gizmo was struggling under the weight of his portion of the skeleton and was lagging behind on the railway track.

"Gizmo!" shouted Bob.

"I've got this!" said Lola. Putting on an impressive turn of speed, she raced past Mr. Marcus and scooped up Gizmo.

Just as they cleared the tracks, the barriers of the railway crossing came down.

This didn't stop Mr. Marcus. He turned toward the railway bridge without breaking his stride.

Quick as lightning, Bob barged past Mr. Marcus and blocked him in the middle of the bridge.

Mr. Marcus grabbed for the bone in Bob's mouth, dropping the one that was in his hand.

But Bob was too quick for him and threw the bone in his mouth to Diamond. Mr. Marcus lunged at her, but she was quick too and threw it back to Bob.

Mr. Marcus found himself in an impossible game of monkey-in-the-middle, getting angrier and angrier.

It was then that Bob heard his cue—a noise like a rumble of thunder and then a horn!

In a wily trick he'd learned from playing in the park with Colin, he did a "dummy" throw. Catching Mr. Marcus's eye, he made it look as if he was going to throw the bone in his mouth over the edge of the bridge. In fact, he never let go of it. By the time Mr. Marcus realized this, he'd lost his balance and had toppled over the side of the bridge.

Bob shut his eyes, praying his timekeeping hadn't let him down.

Diamond looked over the side of the bridge as Mr. Marcus landed softly in a container of grain on the midnight freight train.

She started to wag her tail. "It's all right," she said. "You can open your eyes. He's not hurt, just mad!"

"That train's heading for the coast," said Bob. "Where the containers will be put on an enormous cargo ship."

Bob wagged his tail
and then had a thought. "What are
we going to do with the dinosaur
skeleton now?" he asked.

As it happened, Jilly had a
brilliant idea.

Jilly led the way to the village
school. Once in the playground,
she instructed each dog where
to bury its bone.

"The kids are going to have so
much fun finding these," said
Gizmo, burying his in the sandbox.

As the sun began to rise, the Puddle dogs hurried home.

"I wonder what the headline's going to be for tomorrow's paper," said Diamond.

"Doyouthinkhesaurus?!" suggested Bob.

Diamond rolled her eyes.

"What?" asked Bob. "I thought that was a good one!"

———

Mr. Marcus never returned to Puddle. In fact, no one in the village ever heard from him again. His shop became the Curiosity Bookshop, and its new owner was more than happy to adopt Diamond.

Diamond and Bob are great friends and meet every morning at eleven o'clock in Pageant Gardens for their daily walk. They've decided to make Dinosaur Day Diamond's official birthday.

Don't miss

THE DAILY BARK

THE PUPPY PROBLEM

THE ADVENTURES OF

PUG!

AVAILABLE NOW

Read all Fabio's adventures

Available now

About the Author and Illustrator

LAURA JAMES lives near Bath, England, with her two writing companions, wire-haired dachshunds Brian and Florence. They are a constant source of inspiration for her stories, and she adores their every bark, tail-wag, and tummy-rub request. Sometimes she wonders if they might secretly be writing about her too! She is also the author of the Pug and the Fabio the World's Greatest Flamingo Detective series.

CHARLIE ALDER lives in Devon, England, with her husband and son. When not drawing chickens or dogs, Charlie can be found in her studio drinking coffee, arranging her crayons, and inventing more accidental animal heroes. She also illustrates the Doggo and Pupper series by Katherine Applegate.